The Potato Story

and Other Missionary Stories for Children

Compiled from past issues of *The Alliance World* (a missionary education tool published by Christian Publications)

Illustrated by Elynne Chudnovsky

CHRISTIAN PUBLICATIONS / Camp Hill, Pennsylvania

The mark of vibrant faith

Christian Publications
3825 Hartzdale Drive, Camp Hill, PA 17011

© 1992 by Christian Publications. All rights
reserved.
ISBN: 0-87509-484-8
LOC Catalog Card Number: 91-78295
Printed in the United States of America

92 93 94 95 96   5   4   3   2   1

Contents

The Potato Story

Nema sighed as she lifted the heavy pail of water down from her head. This trip to the well had been more difficult than usual. Most days when she went early in the morning, her neighbor Yainde would not be there yet, but today she was. Yainde was Nema's enemy.

It was not easy being the only Christian in her village. Every Sunday morning Nema would rise early to get her housework taken care of, and then she would set off on the two-mile walk to the next village to meet with a small group of believers. They were the only real friends she had now that she had become a Christian. Most people in her village tolerated her and her new beliefs, and they let her live in peace. But Yainde was different—Yainde hated her.

When Nema accepted the Lord Jesus into her life as Savior, she experienced a joy that was greater than anything she had ever imagined. She was so excited about what happened that she wanted to tell everyone she knew about it. One of the people she told was Yainde.

Yainde was not a happy woman. Life had not been kind to her, and as a result she had become bitter and angry. When she saw the joy of the Lord that shone on Nema's face, it contrasted so with her own inner turmoil that it made her angrier than ever.

So Yainde had resolved to make life miserable for Nema. And to a large extent she had succeeded. She would ridicule Nema at every opportunity, and she sent kids in to steal things from her yard. Once she even tripped Nema as she came back from the well, causing her to spill a pail of cold water down her back. But Nema kept trying to witness to Yainde. It was evident that if anyone needed the Lord, this angry neighbor did.

One day Nema met Yainde at the market. Yainde was grumbling loudly as she went from stall to stall in the marketplace. "Look at this stuff!" she exclaimed to Nema. "In just one week the price of tomatoes and peanuts has increased by half! How on earth are we supposed to feed our families if the prices continue to rise like this? We are going to starve to death! What will we do?"

Nema nodded and replied, "Yes, times are getting hard. It is certainly difficult to find enough money to buy food. And yet, for those of us who believe in Jesus, we have the assurance that He will take care of us. God's word tells us that He will keep those who hope in Him alive in times of famine. I believe that promise, so I am not afraid."

Yainde's face contorted with rage. "You and your Jesus! I have had enough! I am sick and tired of hearing it all!" And with a sudden movement she reached down into the wares of a nearby vendor, snatched up a potato and furiously hurled it at Nema!

The potato hit Nema on the cheek with a resounding smack. Startled, she gasped as tears of pain came into her eyes. She didn't say a word, but in her heart she prayed that the Lord would help her respond in a manner that would honor Him. As she stood there,

humiliated and wanting to run, she saw the potato lying on the ground near her feet.

Slowly she bent over and picked it up. She held it in her hand and looked at it thoughtfully. "Lord," she prayed, "please show me how I can use this potato to show Yainde how much you love her."

After paying the surprised vendor for it, Nema placed the potato in her basket and headed for home. As she walked, she thought and thought. And just as she entered the gate to her courtyard, an idea came to her.

Quickly she put away her market things, dressed in her work clothes, gathered up her gardening tools and hurried out to her garden. It was planting season, and the Lord had given her an idea about what to do with the potato.

Nema carefully prepared the soil and then took the potato in her hand to cut it up for planting. It was a large potato with many eyes, and Nema knew that if she cut it up and planted it, a new potato plant would grow from each piece with an eye. And so Nema planted the pieces of potato, praying as she did so that the Lord would give her a bountiful crop.

For many weeks Nema watched over her garden and did everything she knew to care for it. Little green shoots came up, and before long large plants were flourishing. Nema watered and weeded and waited for the potatoes to grow.

When the time to harvest the potatoes arrived, Nema dug them up carefully. She wanted every one of those potatoes to be the best that it could possibly be. And they were beautiful! She got a whole big basket of them.

Nema returned to her house and prepared to go visiting. She washed and put on her best clothes. Then she lifted the heavy basket of potatoes and set it on her head.

Walking through the village, she soon came to Yainde's house. She clapped and called a greeting. "*Yainde, po!*

Yainde, po!"

Yainde heard her voice and muttered to herself, "That's Nema! What could she want?" Yainde didn't really want to answer the door. But she knew it was terribly rude not to do so, and so grudgingly she answered, *"Owo, gin daw. We yo,"* inviting Nema to come in.

After exchanging greetings, Nema lowered the basket from her head. "I've brought you a gift," she said. Yainde looked startled. What on earth could this woman be bringing her? Gifts were a sign of friendship, but she had certainly been no friend to Nema.

Nema gestured toward the basket. "These potatoes are for you," she said.

"Do you remember that day in the market when you got so angry that you picked up a potato and threw it at me?"

Yainde grimaced. "Yes, I remember. I . . . I really wasn't very nice that day. I was furious with you, and my anger got the best of me."

"Well," Nema answered, "I wanted to show you that God loves you. And because He lives in me and I am His child, I can love you, too—even after what happened that day in the market.

"I took the potato you threw at me, cut it up and planted it, and it has produced all these potaoes. They are yours. I brought them here as a gift."

Yainde didn't know what to say.

5

What kind of God was this that could enable a person to repay good for evil? Maybe this Jesus could change her life, too.

And so that day Yainde listened willingly to the story of Jesus. Before too long she was going with Nema on Sunday mornings to hear God's Word preached at the little church in the next village. And one day Yainde understood that Jesus could change her life, and she asked Him to do so.

That was a joyful day, a day that made the pain and humiliation of the potato hitting her face worth it all to Nema. Now there are two Christians in her village—perhaps soon there will be more.

The Wanderer

Raul was born in the high Andes Mountains of Peru. I think he shivered at night because of the cold winds in those mountains. But cold weather wasn't his worst trouble. Raul's mother and father died and he had to live at his grandmother's. Probably you have a very kind grandmother, but Raul's grandmother was a very unkind woman. She did not like Raul and did not want him to live with her. So life was not very easy or happy for him.

One day, when Raul was seven years old, he was walking around his village picking up stones and throwing them at targets to see how good his aim was. A neighbor's pig happened to walk by and Raul took aim and threw a large rock at the pig. The stone hit the pig in just the right spot and it fell over dead. Raul was horrified! He knew his grandmother would give him a terrible beating when she found out about it.

Raul was so scared he didn't think clearly. He decided that he better get on the other side of the river away from his grandmother. He ran to the river and jumped in hoping to swim across. But he had forgotten that the river was

dangerously high at that time. The cold, swift current took Raul like a rubber ball and bounced him far down the river. He couldn't get across; he couldn't touch bottom. And he could just barely get a breath now and then to keep alive. On and on the freezing water took him. Finally he was able to struggle out, more dead than alive.

Raul was shivering from his terrible river ride. He crawled under a bush but had nothing to warm himself with. For nearly an hour he lay shivering there, his teeth chattering. He didn't know it then, but he was catching pneumonia. As he lay there near death, an old lady who lived in a hut along the side of the river came walking by. She noticed something under a bush and found that it was a sick little boy. Somehow she got Raul to her poor little cabin and she began to take care of him.

After a couple of weeks he was well again and the old lady said to him, "Raul, I cannot keep you here. I hardly have enough food to keep myself alive. You will have to leave." So this seven-year-old boy, who owned nothing, had to leave this kind woman's house.

As he wandered around he eventually came to a mining village. At that time there were no laws in Peru about children working. Some mine bosses hired boys to go into the low tunnels to pick up the ore, put it into leather bags and drag it out of the mine. A lot of boys were doing this kind of work in the mine that Raul had come across, so he was able to get a job there. He was a strong boy and a bit large for his age, so he managed to do this hard work.

Later, an American engineer who worked at this mine noticed Raul and gave him a job as an errand boy in the office. This was much easier, but it made the other boys very jealous of Raul. These boys all lived together in a dormitory and they would often pick on Raul because of this job. But because of his size, Raul was able to take care of himself in these fights.

One day the engineer told Raul, "Raul, I am going back to the United States. I have no family and I have come to love you like a son. I would like to adopt you and make you my son and give you an education." Up until now Raul had never been to school.

The other boys found out about this and because of their jealousy they began to tell Raul wild stories. One of these stories was that in the United States they eat little boys. Another was that the man would make Raul his slave. Raul became very confused. He liked the man very much, but what if these stories were true? He didn't know what to do. One day he just packed his few things and ran away. Raul never saw that man again.

For quite a few years Raul wandered from place to place. Sometimes he would find work in a mine or on a farm. But there was no one to tell him how to behave or to love him as parents would, so he grew into a very rough young man. When he reached the age of 18, he was living down on the coast of Peru. He was large and husky and the leader of a very tough gang. These boys beat up people and stole from them, so everyone was afraid of them.

One Sunday when this gang was roaming around, they saw a group of young people having a street meeting, telling others about Jesus. A young woman about 16 years old was telling the people what Jesus had done for her. Raul said to his gang, "Aha, here's where we'll have some fun. Let's break this up!" They found some rotten vegetables and began throwing them at the young people. But they just kept right on with their meeting.

Raul said, "OK, I'll take care of this." He pushed his way through the crowd and went right up to where the young woman was standing. He just stood right in front of her. She ignored him and kept right on talking. Raul, who was smoking a cigarette, blew the smoke in her face. The woman was quoting from Matthew 11:28. "Come unto me, all you who are weary and burdened, and I will give you rest."

To Raul these words seemed to come straight from God. He couldn't understand what was happening, but he felt something sharp in his heart. Without another word he turned and left the girl, left the crowd, left his friends and went straight to his room. There, still not understanding what was happening, he got down on his knees and prayed, "God, if there is a God, if You can do anything with a wretched life like mine, I pray that You will change me."

God answered that prayer and Raul was saved. God certainly changed him!

He left his gang and began to go with those young people to tell others about Jesus. People were amazed when they saw this man who used to be so rough speaking for Jesus.

Later he started taking God's Word into many parts of Peru. Sometimes he was put in prison for selling Bibles—which was illegal in Peru then. In prison, Raul would talk to the police and jailkeepers. Soon they would be on their knees accepting Christ as their personal Savior and so the authorities would let Raul out.

Raul kept on telling people about Jesus—including his own children, all of whom became useful to God.

The Secret Hideaway

Do you have a secret hiding place where you like to go to think? Is it in the attic? Is it among the branches of a tree in your backyard? It's nice to be alone in your own special place. You can play house, read books, play with cars or take a nap. You can also talk to God in your hiding place, can't you? Today we are going to hear about someone else who had a secret hideaway. Her name was Nonabah Williams. She was a Navajo Indian. She lived and went to school in California.

One day while she was at school, a young missionary spoke to the class. This woman told the children very plainly that Jesus loved them and that He gave His life so that they could know Him. This was the first time Nonabah heard the gospel. She began to think about what the missionary had said. Instead of playing with her friends, she slipped quietly into her secret hideaway. Do you know where her hideaway was? I'll tell you where it was! She loved to hide in the bottom of a big old tree that was hollowed out. There

she could be quiet and think about the special message she heard.

Deep down inside Nonabah wanted to give her heart to Jesus. She wanted to belong to Jesus. In her hideaway she spoke to Him, even though she didn't know Him as her Savior yet. It seemed to her as though the Lord just put His hand in hers and said, "I want you for my child."

One day Nonabah was with her best friend, Rose. Nonabah said, "Rose, when the missionary comes again, I am going to go forward to the altar and give my heart to the Lord."

"Are you really? That's a big decision. What will your Navajo friends think?"

"It doesn't matter what they think. I know that I need to give my life to Jesus so that I can tell my Navajo people about the God who can save His people from their sins." Nonabah knew many of her Navajo people didn't know Jesus, and she wanted to take the Bible to them and teach them about her Friend.

At the next missionary service, there were almost 2,000 students in the auditorium. That's a lot of people! When the missionary asked if anyone wanted to give his or her heart to Jesus, Nonabah stood up before the Lord and gave her life to Jesus. "Lord Jesus, whatever You want, wherever You lead, I will follow You," she said.

Soon Nonabah heard footsteps behind her. She looked up and saw it was her friend Rose. They both signed cards which were a reminder that they had promised to live their lives for Jesus. Nonabah kept the card and placed it on her mirror at home to remind her every day of the promise she made to Jesus.

Not too long after Nonabah became a follower of Jesus, she became very ill. She had a serious disease called tuberculosis. At that time, there was no medicine to cure the disease. Fourteen different doctors examined Nonabah. They all shook their heads and told her that her condition was very poor. They said she needed to go to a special hospital or she would die in less than four weeks.

But Nonabah didn't worry. She remembered one more doctor—the Great Physician, Jesus. She believed He would care for her and heal her body. She went home and her parents took very good care of her. It was good to see their smiles and know that they knew Jesus' love. Together they prayed every day for Nonabah to be healed of the disease. Soon Nonabah became stronger and stronger. Jesus healed her of the tuberculosis!

One day Nonabah met one of the doctors who had said she would die. He was amazed to see her. "What kind of medicine did you take to make you well—the medicine man's medicine?" he asked.

"No," Nonabah said. "Jesus Christ made me well."

Nonabah finished school and became a missionary to the Navajo Indians. She loved her people, but she loved Jesus more and wanted her friends to know Him, too.

A Bowl of What?

It was a beautiful, sunny morning as missionaries Tony Bollback and Fred Ruhl climbed into the big, old mission truck and headed out of town.

Bouncing along the bumpy road on their way to Changsha, they munched happily on the donuts Mrs. Bollback had sent along. In a few hours they would be with the Christians at the Changsha Chinese church.

All at once, they noticed that the sunny sky was turning dark. It began to rain. The harder it rained, the muddier the road got. The ruts became so deep that Fred had to drive very slowly to not damage the truck.

"It shouldn't be long now until we get to Changsha," Fred assured Tony several hours later. "We're finally at the river. Changsha is just a few miles."

Tony had not been in China very long. This was his first trip to Changsha, and it was turning out to be much longer than he had planned.

As the missionaries pulled up to the river's edge, Tony was shocked to see the bridge. It certainly wasn't a bridge like he was used to in America. This bridge was only two boards laid across big wooden beams. And there were no guardrails on the sides. Fred would have to make sure that one tire was on one board and the other tire on the other board and drive very straight so they wouldn't fall into the river.

"The water is quite high," Fred cautioned Tony. "Before we go across, I think you better walk out onto the bridge to make sure it isn't washed out in the middle."

Tony pulled his jacket around him as he crawled out of the truck and into the blowing rain. Following the path of the headlight beams, he edged toward the center of the bridge. It was good that he was watching where he was going because in the middle of the bridge a large section was missing! It had dropped off into the rushing water below.

Tony and Fred realized that it would be impossible to reach Changsha that night. They were both very tired and very hungry. Now what would they do?

"Let's go back to the farmhouse we passed," suggested Fred. "Maybe they will give us food and a place to stay."

In response to the missionaries' knock at the farmhouse, an old woman opened the door.

"Come in," she said in Chinese as she welcomed them into the dimly lit room.

The family was very friendly and soon offered to make something to eat.

Tony looked at Fred.

"Boy, that's what we really need," he said in English. "A good hot meal! I'm starved!" They smiled their appreciation to the grandmother.

One of the younger women went to a dark corner of the room and started stirring some food in a big frying pan called a wok. Soon a wonderful smell filled the house. The missionaries could hardly wait to eat.

The grandmother invited the men to sit at the small table in the middle of the room where a bowl of steaming food was set before them. Although it was so dark that they couldn't see what they were eating, it sure tasted good.

"Thank you very much," they told the cook. "We were so hungry and that tasted so good."

When they finished eating, the grandmother called to some boys sitting along the wall.

"Take these doors off their hinges," she told them. "We will make a bed out of the doors for our guests to sleep on."

Everyone obeyed the grandmother, and soon the missionaries were crawling into their sleeping bags. It didn't seem to matter that the doors didn't make a very soft bed—the missionaries were soon sound asleep.

They woke up the next morning to find it was still raining.

"You know that the bridge has been out," the grandmother said. "We haven't been able to get to the market for food. But we would be glad to make you breakfast if you don't mind eating the same thing you had last night."

"Oh, that will be fine," Tony responded. "That was some of the most delicious food I have ever eaten."

The young woman beamed with pride as once more she cooked and stirred in the corner of the room.

The men pulled up to the table as their meal was set before them. What a surprise! There, right in front of their very eyes, was a bowl full of minnows—tiny little fish complete with heads and eyes and tails!

Fred and Tony glanced at each other. Suddenly, what had tasted so good in the dark the night before, did not look so delicious. How could they possibly eat a big bowl full of minnows?

The missionaries remembered that God wants His children to be thankful in every situation. So they decided not to look, but just to eat and be thankful.

Down went the minnows!

The Bible says, *"No matter what happens, always be thankful, for this is God's will for you who belong to Christ Jesus"* (1 Thessalonians 5:18 LB).

Don't Look at the Mask

Ahou rolled over on her mat. She tried to draw her *pagne* (wrap) up around her head to keep the mosquitoes from biting. She could hear the fetish drums beating not far away. Tonight some of the village men were holding a secret fetish dance. A hideous masked figure would come out and dance around the village. No woman or girl was permitted to watch. Ahou knew that most of the village believed that if a female saw the mask, she would die.

Her friend, Amuen, didn't believe that. She was a Christian. Her God was more powerful than any other, she said. She had even dared to watch the mask dance the last time it had come out. And she wasn't dead! Ahou had often wondered if it was one of the villagers who danced, but she didn't dare voice this thought. Amuen, however, said she knew who it was! She had looked around the audience and figured out who wasn't there.

Thoughts whirled through Ahou's mind. If the mask could really kill women and girls who watched it, why

was Amuen still alive? Was her God really more powerful than the fetish mask? Amuen's family had even burned all their protective charms and idols. They trusted only their God to protect them!

Suddenly the beat of the drums intensified until she could feel the pulse. The mask was dancing right in front of the house. Ahou's heart kept time with the pounding drum as she moved to the window. Her hand was on the shutter when her mother entered the room. "Ahou! What are you doing? You surely aren't going to look at the mask!"

Ahou considered telling a lie, but realized that her mother would never believe that she had wanted a breath of fresh air. No matter how hot it got, the family always slept with their windows closed. After all, you never knew what spirits were roaming the village at night. "Mother, haven't you ever wanted to see the mask? Amuen saw it and she's fine."

Her mother shook her head. "Amuen is foolish. She will surely bring the wrath of the spirits on herself. Don't you ever try to do the things that are forbidden. The power of the spirits is great, and you will bring sorrow to us all."

Ahou sank down on her mat and drew her *pagne* around her. Her mind was a jumble of fear, curiosity and despair.

The sun was barely up when the swish of the broom and the rooster's crowing awakened Ahou. She hurried to help her mother fetch water for baths. Usually on Sundays, Ahou's family went to work in their fields. Today was different, however. There was going to be a funeral in the village, and they were all expected to attend. Manmin Aya, a wise old woman, had died two months ago and had been buried immediately. Her funeral then had to be organized. Word had gone out announcing the funeral, and everyone who had known her was expected to attend. They would spend the time eating, drinking palm wine and dancing so that Manmin Aya's spirit would be satisfied and would find rest peacefully.

"Hello," Amuen called out as she passed by Ahou's house. After exchanging news, Amuen said, "Come with me to church." Ahou wanted to go, but her mother's words put fear into her, and she refused.

When Ahou's family had dressed and eaten a quick breakfast of toasted yams, they walked toward the center of the village. A large bamboo shelter with a palm leaf roof had been built there for the occasion. "Father," Ahou asked, "can the fetishes protect us from everything?"

"Well," her father answered, "I have many fetishes that protect us from many things. I have these rings. This one protects me from gunshots, and that one protects me from car accidents. This other one saves me from knife wounds, and these amulets guard against sickness."

Ahou considered this and then said, "Manmin Aya had lots of fetishes, and she even had a relative who was a witch doctor. She often gave sacrifices of chickens and goats, but she died!"

"Yes, but there are no rings or fetishes to protect against death," answered her father. He picked up a drum and began to play it, keeping rhythm with the chanting.

As soon as she could, Ahou left the dancing crowd and ran down the narrow path toward the church. She timidly entered and an usher squeezed her onto one of the backless benches. The people were singing songs about God and His power over Satan. They were singing that God was eternal—that He never died. Everyone clapped the rhythm as they sang, and they played drums. Then a man got up to speak. He told how he had feared death before he had become a child of God. He explained that all people had sinned or done wrong things that separated them from God. Then God sent His own Son Jesus to be the sacrifice for their sins.

Ahou had never heard of such a great sacrifice before. The best sacrifice in the village was a cow, but only the wealthy could afford that! God must have really cared a lot to give His only Son as a sacrifice. The pastor explained how Jesus had been buried and how three days later He came alive again! "No one can do that," thought Ahou. But as she listened, she heard that God had promised that those who believed in Him would rise and never die. They too would live forever!

After church, Ahou asked if Amuen would tell her what to do so that she could live forever. "You have to believe that Jesus is God's Son and that He died for you. You have to confess that you are a sinner, and you have to ask Jesus to forgive you. Then you have to change your way of life and follow God. He will provide and take care of you."

After praying with the pastor, Ahou and Amuen started back to the village. Ahou knew it would not be easy to tell her parents about her decision, but she knew that God would protect and help her. She was truly free!

Escape from Vietnam

Toan had a secret! For three months Toan prayed every morning about his secret. He only talked to God about the secret—never to his friends or family. His secret was very important. He could not tell anyone or it would be ruined.

Do you want to know what Toan's secret was? Toan wanted to leave his home country, Vietnam. He wanted to go to a camp in the Philippines where there were many Vietnamese refugees. There were 100 new Christians in that refugee camp, but there was no leader or pastor to help these young Christians grow in Christ. Toan wanted so much to go to the camp and help these new Vietnamese Christians grow in Jesus.

Toan had a big problem. He didn't have any money to pay for such a trip. Even if he had the money, however, the communist government would not let him leave Vietnam. But Toan had faith in God. So he prayed morning and evening asking God to direct him.

One day a man visited Toan. He had come to ask Toan to help him escape

Vietnam! How could Toan help some-one else when he needed help himself? This visitor had four young children and part of the plan for escaping from the country meant the children would have to be carried out to a boat. Toan was a strong man and would be able to do such a job. The visitor offered to pay Toan's fare if Toan would go with him.

Was this God's answer to Toan's secret prayers? He wasn't sure. He felt excited, but he also felt concerned. You see, Toan had a wife and two-year-old daughter. Would he have to leave them in Vietnam?

Toan told the man he would have to pray about this big decision. Toan and the visitor said goodbye. Toan quickly went to talk to his wife. How surprised she must have been! This was the first she had even heard about his secret re-quest to the Lord! Of course she wanted the family to stay together, so she began to pray with Toan that they would all be able to leave Vietnam together.

They didn't have to wait long for an answer! In two days the man came back with good news. The visitor told Toan that there was a boat that would take Toan and his family out of Vietnam. Toan would not have to pay any money until he and his family were resettled in another country. How they thanked God for this blessing.

As joyful as Toan and his wife were about escaping from Vietnam, they were sad, too. They had relatives and many friends in Vietnam. Most likely Toan and his wife would never see their families again. Toan also knew that the journey would be very dangerous; however, he was convinced that God was leading them.

Just two hours before they left, Toan shared the secret with his in-laws and his pastor. Can you imagine the hugs and tears of that little group as they quickly said goodbye and boarded the bus?

Although the bus was made to hold only 50 people, more than 100 crowded aboard. Some people sat on others' shoulders and some settled in the aisle. Many of the people had fearful looks on their faces. They were thinking about the many checkpoints they would have to pass. If the communist soldiers saw them at the checkpoints with the small bags of food and medicine, the soldiers would know they were trying to escape and all would be lost. Yet miraculously they made the journey without interruption.

It was late at night when they reached their meeting point. In fact, it was too late! The boat had left! They learned that it would return the next night, but where could they wait? They decided to go south about 50 miles. This was risky. They knew it would take just one soldier to find where they were hiding. But God was with Toan. He protected Toan and his family. No one bothered them all day.

When Toan and the rest of the group returned the next night, they found they were too early. No boat was in sight. Some of the people began to cry. Toan decided to swim out into the ocean and try to find the boat. He and another man jumped into the dark water. It was so black they could hardly see their hands in front of their faces. After swimming several hundred yards they still had not found the boat. They wondered if they should return to shore. Just then—bump! What had they touched in the darkness? Yes! It was exactly what they were looking for—their boat to freedom.

Now, all those refugees had to get through the water and onto the boat. Some couldn't swim, and it was, of course, still very dark. They didn't dare use lights. They knew of other people who had died in attempts to get from the shore to the boat.

Toan's wife and little girl and sister-in-law were in a small basket boat paddling over this stretch of ocean. None of them could swim. As they got to the boat and were helped over the side, Toan knew again that God was answering his prayer.

All of the refugees reached the boat safely. As a little light came into the sky, they checked the compass to make sure they were going in the right direction. The compass was broken! I'm sure it was the Lord who reminded Toan to use the sun as a direction guide. The crew set to sea, heading for the Philippines.

They had no way of knowing how long they would be on the open sea. Toan had heard stories of some refugees who sailed for over a month. So they rationed their water and food.

On the second day at sea they spied a large ship in the distance. As the ship came closer, they realized it was painted red. Was it a Russian ship? Would it take them back to Vietnam? No—it was a West German scientific research ship.

At first the captain of the German ship said he could not take the refugees aboard. He offered to give them food and gas, but that was all. One of the Christians pleaded their case! He explained that there were many children and women on the boat. If sea pirates should find them, they would be treated horribly. Finally the captain agreed to take them aboard!

Toan watched as the refugees climbed from their little boat onto the huge ship. A rope ladder was put over the side and each person had to climb about 80 feet up along the side of the ship. Climbing the ladder was difficult because it was made of rope. Toan held the ropes below to keep the ladder from hitting the ship. He watched as his wife and little daughter were the first to climb up slowly and crawl across the top rail. What relief and joy he felt as they made it safely. He patiently helped as others went up. Then, with no one to hold the rope, Toan climbed up the ladder.

Two and a half days later the giant ship and all of the refugees pulled into the harbor of Manila in the Philippines. From there they were taken to the refugee camp. Toan wasted no time. He immediately began teaching the new Christians. He wanted to stay as long as possible to help them grow into strong believers!

A Vietnamese church in Canada heard about Toan and his family. They wanted to help bring Toan to Canada where he could live in peace and safety. You see, the refugee camp in the Philippines is not a place where Toan could make his home. The camp is only a stopping place to help refugees until another country will bring them in to stay. Through the Vietnamese church and the safekeeping of God, Toan and his family finally arrived in Canada. They were free at last.

A Flood of Trouble

It was a perfect place! Christian and his family were delighted with the camping spot their father had picked. It was close to a clear rushing stream, had plenty of shade, rocks to climb and not many other campers around. This was a lovely part of Argentina.

Christian helped his father, Justo, stabilize the camper. With his three sisters, he looked forward to every chance he had to be with his dad. Justo was a very busy lawyer, so going on a vacation where they could spend time with him was a treat for his family.

The sun was setting as they finished all the preparations. Justo looked anxiously at the sky. "It looks like a bad storm is blowing up," he said. Christian's family carefully secured everything in case there would be a bad storm. Then they went to bed. It wasn't long before the wind began to blow very hard and the rain pelted down.

Justo went to the door of the camper and looked out. He couldn't believe his eyes! He could see water under the camper. Just a short while ago there had been a lovely mountain stream nearby. Now there was a raging river flooding the whole area.

"Oh, Justo!" His wife Marta gasped. "What are we going to do?"

Christian trembled in his cot. Just then they heard shouts and Justo could see some lights flashing through the rain. It was a group of policemen who had come to get the girls. They told Christian to get his heavy coat. They were going to wade through the water to higher ground.

The next morning Justo and the policemen went to see how high the water was and if Justo could get the car and camper out. Christian's heart sank as he heard his father talking to his mother.

"The water is over the bumper," he said. "But the policemen think I can drive it out because the car has a big engine and is well-built."

"Oh, Justo," Marta pleaded. "Don't take chances. Please! You might be swept away down the river."

"I'll be careful," Justo replied calmly. "I have to try and get the car out."

Christian watched as his father walked down the hill toward the river with the policemen. He couldn't imagine what would happen to them if something happened to his father. Christian ran down the road in the direction his father had gone. When he got to the water, Christian could see the car inching through the water, dragging the camper. The water was so deep, the car made waves like a boat. *How could the motor even run?* Christian wondered.

Christian watched in horror as the front end of the car suddenly went under water. A wave went over the entire car! His father would never get out of there alive! Christian closed his eyes in terror.

But the engine kept on running. Justo kept plowing through the water. Finally, it became shallow. Soon he was up on dry land again. Christian ran to him and threw his arms around him.

The policemen began congratulating his father. "One thing is sure," one of them said to Justo. "You not only have a great car, but you have nerves of steel and a good God looking out for you."

Justo laughed. "You're right about the car and my nerves," he said. "But if there is a God, He's going to have to show Himself to me in some way I can understand."

Christian listened curiously. His father *never* talked about God! Christian figured lawyers didn't need God, and he was sure his father didn't.

The family was so upset that they went home to Buenos Aires right away, ending their vacation. But at home, things continued to go badly for them. The doctors told them Christian's little sister, Erika, would never be normal and would probably never be able to talk. This news made Christian's mother feel so sad that she went to bed and stayed there. Sometimes Marta wouldn't even turn over and drink the cups of tea Christian took to her.

Several months went by like this. Some days were better than others for Marta, but Christian hated to go home after school. Most of the time he found his mother sad and the house a mess. Christian and his sisters tried not to let anyone know about the problems they had at home.

And Christian's father was having problems, too. He had a health problem that was getting worse and worse and would soon require surgery. But how could he go into the hospital with Marta ill? Who would take care of the children? Finally, one day, he slumped down into a chair and told the children that he really didn't know what to do.

Christian felt fear in his heart. What would they do if something happened to his father? He tried to comfort his father and tell him that they would be fine, but deep down, Christian knew there was no hope if his father got sick.

A couple of days later, a friend talked to Justo about some special meetings that were going on in a tent near where they lived. "You should go," he said. "People even get healed at those meetings!"

Justo had heard about the meetings, but he made fun of the people who went there. He certainly didn't want to go. But the friend's suggestion wouldn't leave his mind and he suddenly decided to go to one of the meetings and take Erika with him. *After all,* he thought, *it can't do any harm, so I might as well try it.*

That night Justo and Erika went to the meeting. There were no benches to sit on. People just stood outside, crowded together. The singing was loud and there was a lot of clapping and shouting. Justo felt very strange being there. He held Erika tightly and listened to what the preacher said. The speaker made it very clear that all men were sinners, but that God loved them and had provided a way of salvation through His Son, Jesus Christ. He asked everyone to pray and he began to pray for all the sick people standing there, that God would heal them.

Justo noticed a strange feeling of warmth in his body. That night Justo responded for the first time in his life to a God he had never believed in. He felt completely different. When he got home, Justo excitedly told Marta and the children about his experience. The family listened to him, amazed. Christian had never heard his father talk like that before.

The most amazing thing happened the next day when Justo went back to the doctors. They told him that his problem had completely disappeared! Justo knew God had healed him, and he told the shocked doctors, too.

Seeing the changes in her husband made Marta feel she needed God in her life. One day, Marta asked a friend if she knew of any churches nearby.

The friend thought a minute and then said, "There's an evangelical church just a few blocks from here. I pass it all the time." She gave Marta the address and Marta went to one of the services at the church. Marta listened to what was preached that night and she liked it. Before long Pastor Rogelio Nonini led her to the Lord.

Justo gladly went with his happy wife to the services at the church. The whole family began attending and the children became a part of the Sunday school. Christian began to think seriously about his own life and his need of God. One night he opened his heart to Jesus and became a child of God—Christian became a Christian.

The Mysterious Water Witness

Can you guess what a mysterious water witness might be? You are going to find out how God used the Dantiwada Alliance Church in Gujarat State, India, to witness for Him.

What does it mean to "witness" for the Lord?

Before Jesus went back to heaven, He told the disciples to go and tell people about Him. But Jesus was not just talking to the disciples, He was talking to us, too. What are we supposed to tell others about Him? As Christians, we are supposed to tell people about Jesus. We are to tell them how He came and died on the cross so that we can have eternal life with God in heaven.

It's pretty scary to talk to someone about Jesus, especially if that person becomes angry. I don't know about you, but I don't think I can do that by myself.

How does Jesus expect us to do it? Jesus sent the Holy Spirit to give us the power to witness for Him. So we don't have to do it on our own.

To witness, you don't have to jump up on a platform and preach or be a

famous singer or a teacher or a speaker. There's nothing wrong with being someone like that, but most witnessing is done by just being you: sharing what Jesus has done for you, living like Jesus told us to live and being willing to help people when they need it. Witnessing might be as simple as carrying a sloshing bucket of water for your neighbor.

Buckets of water were a way for the Dantiwada church in Gujarat, India, to witness. The land the church sat on did not have a city water supply. They could not run pipes to the nearest street to hook up with the city water pipes.

Next door, a Hindu man busily worked on building his house. City water did not concern him, because he had a well filled with plenty of water.

The same builder was working on both the church and this man's house, so he decided to pour the concrete for the roof slabs, at the same time.

The neighbor had been politely allowing the Dantiwada pastor to draw water from his well for personal use, such as drinking. Being a Hindu, he was not happy about seeing a Christian church being built right next door, but he tried to be nice about it. That is, until . . .

"You know it takes a great deal of water to mix with cement for the roof of a building. May we have your permission to draw water from your well when we are ready to do our roof slab?" the pastor asked.

"No," the man answered. "That takes too much water, and I may need all of the water myself."

His refusal left the Dantiwada pastor and the Palanpur pastor, who was helping, no choice but to arrange for four or five workers to carry water from a well that was quite a long distance away.

The day the two roof slabs were to be poured, the Hindu contractor in charge of both buildings, came to the pastors. "According to my Hindu religion," he said, "I must offer my rituals and prayers to my gods before I begin this work."

"I'm sorry, but we cannot allow you to perform your rituals on church property," the pastors told him. "We will pray in the name of Jesus that God will bless the work."

"But I cannot proceed without my Hindu rituals!" the contractor exclaimed. "You must let me!"

"We cannot," the pastors replied. "God's Word says it is wrong to worship anyone except Him."

The contractor decided to pour the roof of the neighbor's house first and perform the Hindu rites there.

A worker walked to the man's well and began to pump the handle. Nothing happened!

"I can't get any water," the worker yelled to the owner.

"Pump harder!" the neighbor insisted.

The worker pumped and pumped and pumped. He pumped until his arm hurt, and still no water came.

The Hindu man went over to the church and asked the pastors for help. "My well is dry, and I must have water to mix the cement for my roof slab. Will you help me?"

What do you think the pastors said? "Of course! We'll send the workers we hired to haul our water."

So, the Hindu neighbor, who refused to let his well water be used for pouring the cement for the church roof, had to have all the water carried for his own roof. Carrying two buckets at once for a long distance was hard work, too.

Finally, the neighbor's roof was finished, and the contractor came over to begin work on the church roof. One of the workers decided to try the neighbor's well one more time. Guess what happened? To everyone's amazement, water came! Since the pastors had let their workers help the neighbor carry water, he could not refuse to let them use the water in his well to mix the cement for the church roof.

With a full supply of water, the roof was completed and no one had to carry water for the church.

Did the Christian God really shut off the well water? the Hindu neighbor asked himself.

"There might be something to this Christianity," the contractor told his family.

"Did you hear about what the Christian's God can do?" the other people in the neighborhood asked each other.

God used the mysteriously disappearing well water to help the Christians of the Dantiwada church witness for Him.

Ngoma Learns to Obey

In Zaire, Africa, a baby boy was born to Christian parents. They named him Ngoma. As he grew up, he played in the forest and streams. When he was old enough, he could listen to the beat of the drum and know it was time to go to church. His father was a leader in the church.

Ngoma invited Jesus into his heart when he was 12 years old. Though he liked being a Christian, he didn't want to become a pastor. He thought pastors had too many troubles. He was happy when Jesus did things for him, but he didn't want to do what Jesus asked him to do.

Ngoma's father and the other leaders in the church thought it would be a good idea to send him to Bible school. But Ngoma didn't think so! He was very unhappy about the decision, so he ran away. He left his own village and went to another one. He hoped the people from his home would not come and make him go to Bible school.

The men from Ngoma's village did not follow him, but Someone else was

watching him. Can you guess who? Jesus saw him running away! While Ngoma was at the other village, a strange thing happened. Suddenly he couldn't see. He became blind! It was scary! I wonder if he remembered how Saul was blinded when Jesus talked to him on the road to Damascus? Ngoma probably did because he knew his blindness was a punishment from the Lord.

Ngoma went back to his home village and in just a few days he could see again! He was no longer blind. He could see just as well as before he ran away. He decided that God had let this happen to show him that he should go to Bible school. This time he gave all of his life to the Lord.

While he was at Bible school, Ngoma asked the Lord to show him what kind of work he should do when he finished his studies. He wanted to be like the Apostle Paul who took the gospel to people who had never heard it before. That sounds as though he wanted to be a missionary, doesn't it? Can African churches send out missionaries? Of course!

By now Ngoma was married and had a family. He heard about a place where it was hard to live. One reason it was difficult to live there was that there wasn't much food. He would have trouble feeding his family. The second reason was even worse—the people who lived there served the devil. They put their hope in charms, which they often wore around their necks. They didn't know about God's power. It would be difficult to work in a place like that.

But Ngoma had decided to go God's way. When the African church decided to send a missionary to this difficult place, Ngoma said he would go. He was afraid, but he prayed and asked God to give him courage. God answered his prayer and helped him see how the people were in darkness. Ngoma felt he had to go.

Ngoma's family was taken in a landcruiser—a kind of jeep—to the place where he was going to work. An American missionary and another African missionary went along. The people in the village had no pastor, but they had been meeting every morning and evening to hear God's Word. They were happy to receive Ngoma as their pastor.

It was a special occasion when the village gathered that evening. But soon it looked as if the first service would have to stop. Why? Because it began to rain so hard they thought they would have to stop the service.

Then the other African missionary began to pray, and a miracle happened! The rain stopped! It was exciting that

God allowed Ngoma to continue the service.

God kept on working miracles in the village. People turned to the Lord—that was a miracle. When they did, they burned their charms to show that they no longer served the devil.

Today Ngoma is busy in his village and in others nearby teaching people about Jesus. He is glad he is now obeying God.

For additional copies of *The Potato Story and Other Missionary Stories for Children* or other titles in this series, contact your local Christian bookstore or call Christian Publications toll-free 1-800-233-4443.

Titles available:

Bare, Beautiful Feet and Other Missionary Stories for Children

A Happy Day for Ramona and Other Missionary Stories for Children

The Pink and Green Church and Other Missionary Stories for Children

The Potato Story and Other Missionary Stories for Children